DATE DUE		
JUL 3	OCT 10		PLE
OCT 24			
APR 15			
MAY 5			
APR 28			
SEP 14			
JUL 24			
SEP 5			
SEP 109	/792		

The Bobbsey Twins®

THE MYSTERY OF THE HINDU TEMPLE

LAURA LEE HOPE

Illustrated by Richard Williams

WANDERER BOOKS
Published by
Simon & Schuster, Inc., New York

Manufactured in the United States of America
10 9 8 7 6 5 4 3 2 1

Library of Congress Cataloging in Publication Data

Hope, Laura Lee.
The mystery of the Hindu temple.

(The Bobbsey twins; 13)
SUMMARY: The Bobbsey twins travel to Nepal, where
they become involved in investigating the theft of
valuable Hindu temple treasures.
1. Children's stories, American. [1. Twins—
Fiction. 2. Nepal—Fiction. 3. Mystery and
detective stories] I. Title. II. Series:
Hope, Laura Lee. Bobbsey twins (1980–   ), 13.
P27.H772Mw   Fic   85 –7201
ISBN 0-671-55499-9

Contents

THE MYSTERY OF
THE HINDU TEMPLE

·1·

An Ominous Arrival

"Please be sure your seat belts are fastened," the stewardess announced in Nepali and in English. "We will soon be landing in Kathmandu, Nepal."

The Bobbseys looked excited, then were startled as the airplane echoed with the sound of a goose honking. The man across the aisle from them wiped his nose with a handkerchief, while his attractive, dark-haired wife glared at him.

"I never heard anyone blow their nose so

loud," six-year-old Flossie Bobbsey whispered as she gazed out the window at tall mountains capped with sparkling white snow. Her twin brother Freddie giggled and nodded in agreement.

"Quiet down before he hears you," Mr. Bobbsey said.

The plane landed and taxied down the runway in the small country tucked in the mighty Himalayan mountains. They were now across an ocean and halfway around the world from their home in Lakeport.

"I hope that while you're doing business for the lumberyard," Mrs. Bobbsey said to her husband, "we can find Jeff Jennings. I think his mother is not feeling well because she misses him."

Mr. Bobbsey unbuckled his seat belt as the plane screeched to a halt. "We're not even sure he's in Nepal. His father only guessed that because of the scribbled note he found on the back of an envelope."

"Was it a good-bye note?" twelve-year-old Bert asked.

"No," Mr. Bobbsey replied. "He had told them he was leaving, but he wouldn't say where he was going. I'm sure that the note was left behind accidentally. But it had the words *Kirtipur* and *Kathmandu* written on it."

Slender, dark-haired Nan, Bert's twin sister, looked up. "A clue! That'll help us find him!"

"I hope we can," chubby, blond Freddie said. "Jeff was my good friend!"

"I wonder what Cat-pur means," cute, blond Flossie said.

Mr. Bobbsey affectionately ruffled his daughter's curly hair. "I hope we can soon find out."

They got up to leave the airplane, but the man who had blown his nose loudly and his much-taller wife elbowed them aside and pushed ahead.

"I guess they're in a hurry!" said dark-haired Bert, turning to his parents. "Of course, I hope we find Jeff. But given the situation with his parents, I wonder what's best."

"His mother's sick!" Nan said. "Surely he'll want to go home to see her, if we can just get word to him!"

"I'm sure he will, too," Bert commented. "But you must admit that it's been tough for him at home. His folks didn't let him make any decisions for himself. Why, they wouldn't even let him pick out his own clothes."

"We're old enough for that," Freddie and Flossie giggled. "And we're twelve years younger than Jeff."

Mrs. Bobbsey picked up her purse as they rose from their seats. "I think Mr. Jennings has learned the hard way that he must treat Jeff as an adult. It's certainly time. Jeff is eighteen years old now, hardly a child."

"Now let's hope," Mr. Bobbsey added, "that I can buy the special types of lumber I need for the business, especially the sissoo and sal."

"I never heard of wood like that!" Freddie said.

Mr. Bobbsey smiled. "Of course you haven't. You can't find that in the United States. That's why we had to come so far!"

"We don't mind," Nan and Bert grinned.

"The children and I," Mrs. Bobbsey said, smiling, "will be more than happy to sight-see while you do your business!"

The stewardess stood at the door of the airplane. She wore a sari, her national dress, draped around her. As the Bobbseys left the plane, she clasped her hands in front of her forehead.

"*Namaste*," she said, which was the Nepali greeting. "Have a nice stay in our lovely country."

Flossie clasped her hands and smiled. "*Namaste*," she replied, then whispered to her brother, "See, I know a Nay-plee word!"

They hurried down the ramp in excitement, but were dismayed to see lots of soldiers in light-brown uniforms!

Flossie tossed her blond curls and, walking up to a soldier, clasped her hands in front of her. *"Namaste."*

He frowned back. "Keep moving. You must go to customs."

"What's customs?" she asked.

"That's where we search your luggage!" he shouted. "Move on! Hurry!"

"Everyone looks mad," Freddie said.

"It seems like a lot of soldiers are here," Bert said. "These don't look like ordinary security precautions to me."

"Gosh," Flossie said. "I hope they're not having an revolution."

"We all hope not!" Nan said.

The Bobbseys followed the other airplane passengers through the halls to the customs line. Behind the lines of soldiers stood Nepali citizens, all with angry faces.

"What happened to the other man?" Freddie said. "The one who blew his nose loud?"

"He should be somewhere in this line,"

Mrs. Bobbsey said. "He and his lady friend must go through the customs line. It's the law."

"They're not here," Flossie said. "They must not be going through the line."

"Maybe they don't want to be searched," Freddie said. "I'm hungry. When do we eat?"

Mr. Bobbsey scanned the crowd. "First we have to find Mr. Manadhar, my business contact here."

"How will we know him?" Bert asked.

"He sent a picture of himself," Mr. Bobbsey replied. "And I sent him a picture of us, so he'd recognize us."

Mrs. Bobbsey laughed. "We seem to be the only Americans! And with two six-year-olds, two twelve-year-olds, and two parents, I think we're pretty easy to spot!"

Nan shuddered. "I hope we find him soon. These people don't look very friendly!"

Two young Nepali men ran up to the line

of soldiers. "Americans go home!" they shouted. "American thieves, go home!"

The Bobbseys walked faster and looked nervously at each other.

"Ooo-eee!" Flossie moaned. "This is scary!"

The soldiers tried to quiet the two men, but soon the entire crowd of Nepali cried in unison, "Americans, go home! American thieves, go home!"

·2·

Mysterious Strangers

"You must be the Bobbseys!" said a dark-skinned man in a business suit and a red, brimless hat.

Mr. Bobbsey shook the man's hand. "Durga Manadhar! It's good to meet you. But, please, tell me what's going on here."

"I'm very sorry for the behavior of my countrymen," Mr. Manadhar said. "Follow me to the customs area and I'll explain shortly."

"Do you work in a soda fountain?" Freddie asked as they hurried past the frowning crowds.

"No," Mr. Manadhar replied. "I'm in the lumber business, like your father."

Richard Bobbsey looked at his chubby, blond son. "Why did you ask that?"

"He has a cap like a soda-fountain man," Flossie said.

"Oh!" Mr. Manadhar laughed. "All the men in Nepal wear hats like this."

Freddie patted his camera bag. "Can I take a picture of you?"

"Sure," Mr. Manadhar replied. "But why don't we wait until we reach my house and get out of these crowds?"

"Ooo-eee," Flossie said. "I don't like these crowds. They all look so mean. Is everyone in Nepal so mean?"

Mr. Manadhar sadly shook his head. "Actually, my people are usually very friendly and gentle."

Flossie looked behind her and saw a dark-skinned, dark-eyed boy. "Are you following us?" she asked.

"I'm sorry," Mr. Manadhar said. "In all the confusion, I forgot to introduce my son. This is Mohan. My daughter, Lakshmi, is at home with Devi, my wife. They are fixing a special meal for you."

"Roast beef?" asked Freddie. "That's my favorite!"

"No, no," Mr. Manadhar chuckled. "Our religion is Hinduism, and we do not eat beef, for we believe cows are sacred."

"No roast beef? Ever?" Freddie muttered. "How awful!"

"We wouldn't try it," nine-year-old Mohan said, walking in between Freddie and Flossie. "But if we did, we probably wouldn't like it."

They reached the customs area with long lines of people waiting to be searched. All the Bobbseys were fascinated with watching the people.

"The dresses the women have on," Flossie said, "are beautiful!"

"They're called saris," Mohan Manadhar said.

"I know," Flossie said. "We have a friend, Mrs. Wooley, in Oklahoma, who wears one!"

Freddie and Flossie also envied the many people who were barefoot!

Finally it was the Bobbseys turn to be searched. The official frowned and went through every piece of their luggage, even looking into Mrs. Bobbsey's purse and opening Freddie's camera bag.

"You'll ruin my film," he told the official.

"I have to look," the man grunted, although he did not open the camera. "Valuable objects have been stolen from our Hindu temples. American thieves took them, so we closely search all Americans, even the ones coming *into* the country. We must be extra cautious these days."

"Then we assume," Bert said, "that you searched the other Americans on the plane as thoroughly as you did us."

The man looked up, surprised. "What other Americans?"

"There were two other Americans on the plane," Mrs. Bobbsey explained.

"You must be mistaken," the official said. "You are the only Americans to come through."

"It sounds suspicious," Flossie said.

"Could they have avoided this line?" Bert asked.

"No," the agent said firmly. "That would be impossible. You see, there's no way they can leave the airport without coming through here."

"They were on the plane," Freddie insisted.

"Perhaps," Mr. Manadhar suggested, "you saw light-skinned people and assumed they were Americans."

"They *were* Americans," Nan replied.

"Others are waiting," the official said. "Please move on so others may have their turn."

As they left the airport, Mr. Manadhar told them about the recent rash of thefts. "A young American man has been placed at the scene of the crimes, and anti-American sentiment has been rising."

"That's hardly fair," Nan complained. "We're certainly not the thieves. It's very unfair to take it out on everyone."

"At least I'll get some great pictures here," Freddie said, as a cow strolled across the airport parking lot.

"What kind of valuable objects have been stolen?" Freddie asked Mohan as they walked to the car.

"Religious statues," the boy replied. "They are used for worship. Many of them are worth a lot of money, for they're covered with gold and jewels."

"Wow!" Freddie and Flossie exclaimed. "No wonder your people are so upset!"

Mohan nodded. "The people are mostly angry because of the sacrilege. People plunder our temples, and it makes us sad. Many people fear that God will become angry."

"Are there any clues?" Nan asked, wiping the sweat from her forehead. "Have the police made any progress looking for the thief?"

Mohan shrugged. "I don't know. They're only sure about the American who drives the getaway car. The thieves have been very clever."

"Richard, do you think we should stay here?" Mrs. Bobbsey asked her husband as they reached the car. "The people seem so angry. Suppose there's a revolution?"

"Things could not become that bad," Mr. Manadhar said, opening the door. "I feel sorry that my countrymen have frightened you so."

"The angry crowds are all *inside* the airport," Mr. Bobbsey replied. "I'd just as soon stay out of there. Mr. Manadhar will see that we're safe."

"Yes, I certainly will," Mr. Manadhar said.

Just before they got in the car, Freddie and Flossie noticed a man and woman walking across the parking lot. The man was short and balding, and the woman was very tall, like the couple on the airplane. But they were dark-skinned, and the woman wore a sari, while the man wore a flowing dhoti and the traditional hat.

"I wonder if those are the people who didn't go through customs," Freddie said.

"Yes!" Flossie said excitedly. "They could be the people from the airplane, but now they're in disguise!"

"That's ridiculous," Mr. Bobbsey said. "You children have over-active imaginations. The other people were obviously Americans, and these people obviously are not! Let's get in the car. Mrs. Manadhar is waiting at the house for us."

Freddie got out his camera. "I'll take their picture and prove Flossie's right."

He got out his camera, but the woman saw him.

"*Namaste*," she said, clasping her hands in front of her face.

"Can I take your picture?" Freddie asked.

The man and woman looked back blankly, then hurried away and got into a dark blue car. A driver waited in their car, but shadows hid his face.

"They didn't even speak English," Nan said. "These aren't the people you think they are."

"If they had remained," Mr. Manadhar said, "Mohan and I could have at least translated for them."

"They left because they really do speak English," Freddie insisted. "They're the Americans from the plane."

"You're being silly," Mrs. Bobbsey said,

turning to Mr. Manadhar. "Children have such vivid imaginations."

"Freddie's right," Flossie said, putting her hands on her hips. "Those are the same people. And I think they're up to something funny!"

·3·

A Double Identity

Mr. Manadhar screeched the car to a halt and honked the horn as a cow wandered lazily across the narrow, winding street. When it passed, he started the car again, taking the Bobbseys past wood and stone and earthen houses jammed together. Children played, and women walked along the street carrying large brass jugs on top of their heads.

"Ouch!" Flossie said. "Those women must get awful headaches!"

Mr. Manadhar chuckled. "They do not really get headaches. That is an easy way for them to carry a heavy load."

"Sometimes they put a small pad on top of their head," Mohan added.

"What do they have to carry?" Nan asked.

Mohan waved as they passed a small boy standing in front of a small earthen house. "Many of them are carrying water to their homes."

"How come?" Freddie asked. "Why can't they just turn on their faucets and get it in their houses?"

"Some people have faucets in their homes," Mr. Manadhar said. "For most of the city, however, there are faucets at central locations. The women can go to those and fill their jugs with the water their families need for the day. But in the villages, they must use wells and ponds, for they have no faucets at all."

"How come the men don't carry the water?" Bert asked.

"Women are strong, too," Nan reminded him.

Flossie's eyes opened wide. "No faucets? You don't have faucets at your house? Your wife has to carry all that water every day?"

"Not now," Mr. Manadhar said. "But she used to. However, we are lucky, and we do have running water at our house."

He parked the car in front of a large, square, white house.

"I hope you are hungry," he said, opening the car doors and leading the Bobbseys into the house. "My wife and daughter have been cooking all day long for you!"

A black-haired woman in a sari and a seven-year-old girl in a bright red pinafore shyly greeted them.

Mr. Manadhar proudly pointed to them. "This is Devi, my wife, and my daughter Lakshmi."

The women led them to the dining room table. An aluminum plate had been placed before each seat. Mrs. Manadhar and Lakshmi brought out steaming bowls of food and ladled them onto the plates.

Mrs. Manadhar said something in Nepali to Lakshmi, who turned toward the Bobbseys. "My mother asks me to tell you what our foods are," she said, handing out fried bread. "This is a chapati. And here is rice pulao and dal—lentils— and chicken curry. I hope you enjoy our food."

"My wife does not speak English," Mr. Manadhar explained. "It is only recently that girls have even been allowed to go to school."

Flossie's eyes grew wide and she looked at Lakshmi. "Do you go to school?"

"Yes," Lakshmi replied. "Things are changing now."

"The food smells delicious," Bert said.

"Where's the silverware?" Freddie asked.

Mr. Manadhar laughed. "We do not use it in our country. We break off pieces of the chapati and scoop up our food on it."

"Fewer dishes to wash," Mr. Bobbsey said. "I like that."

Mrs. Bobbsey smiled at her husband. "You notice that more since you began helping with the dishes."

Nan looked at her father. "Dad, maybe the Manadhars could help us figure out Jeff's note." She turned to Mr. Manadhar. "What does the word *Kirtipur* mean?"

"It is a town outside Kathmandu," Mr. Manadhar said.

"We are looking for a friend of our family's," Mr. Bobbsey explained. "He is a nice young man who ran away from home. His father thinks he came to Nepal."

Mr. Manadhar shook his head. "How terrible for a son to leave his parents like that! As if running away could solve anything!"

"It's true, running away can't solve anything," Mrs. Bobbsey said. "It's a sad situation. There were some disagreements between his parents and him, largely because they wouldn't treat him as an adult. Now they're sorry and want to make up, but they can't find him."

"We'll all be happy to help however we can," Mr. Manadhar assured his visitors.

"Our friend goes to school in Kirtipur," Mohan boasted. "He has taught us about the city. I could show you around if you want to look there."

Lakshmi and Mohan also told the Bobbseys that they wanted to show them around Kathmandu. "We would like to introduce you to some of our friends," Lakshmi said. "They'd love to play with you."

"How could we talk to them?" Flossie asked. "We don't speak Nay-plee."

"They all speak English," Mohan replied.

"I noticed," Nan commented, "that the two of you speak English very well."

"We learn a little English in school," Mohan said. "But the real credit belongs to our friend who teaches us. He's the one who goes to school in Kirtipur."

"Yes," Lakshmi said. "He is an American, so we learn . . ."

"An American?" Freddie asked.

"Freddie!" Mr. Bobbsey said. "You shouldn't interrupt."

"I'm sorry," Freddie said. "It's just that . . ."

Flossie bobbed her head up and down. "That was rude of Freddie. It's just that he thinks that . . ."

"I'm sorry," Freddie said to Lakshmi. "I didn't mean to be rude. Please go on."

"We learn English from our friend better than we do in school. After all, our own people don't always know the correct pronunciation of English words."

"Nor do all Americans," Bert said, smiling at his younger sister.

"Did your friends—the ones you want us

to play with—learn English in school?"
Freddie asked.

"They learned as we did," Mohan said.
"Some in school, some from our good friend
Randy Baker."

"He is a very smart man," Lakshmi said.
"I believe he will some day be a scholar, he
is so smart."

Mr. Manadhar nodded. "Yes, he is a fine
young man. He studies and works very
hard. If all Americans are like Randy Baker,
they are fine people indeed!"

"I wish you could meet him," Mohan
told the Bobbseys. "We've not seen much
of him lately. He hardly comes around anymore."

"It's a shame," Mr. Manadhar added,
"because I know you'd enjoy seeing another
of your countrymen."

"Do you know where he is now?" Bert
asked. "I think we'd all enjoy meeting him."

Mr. Manadhar scooped up another helping of chicken curry. "Mohan, perhaps you

could find him and bring him to meet the Bobbseys."

"I tried," Mohan replied. "I went twice to his house looking for him. No one was home, though I left a note."

"I wanted him to look through the window and see if he was there," Lakshmi said. "In case he was at home and couldn't answer."

"I couldn't do that," Mohan said.

"Suppose he's sick?" Lakshmi asked. "He didn't look well the last time we saw him."

"Surely he's okay," Mohan said, turning to the Bobbseys. "He gave us his picture. He said the picture was very special to him, so it's a very special present to us. Would you like to see it?"

"Sure," Freddie and Flossie answered at the same time.

Mohan and Lakshmi got up and dug through a drawer, then returned with a large, framed photograph of an older man and woman and their son. The young man wore a black cap and gown from a high school graduation.

"He has a beard now," Lakshmi explained. "It's so funny to see him in that picture without a beard."

"That's Jeff's pit-cher!" shouted an astonished Flossie. "That's our friend Jeff!"

·4·

Surprise Meeting

Mr. Manadhar's eyes widened with astonishment. "Your friend? Not the one who ran away!"

"This is Jeff," Freddie insisted.

"It's true," Mr. Bobbsey said. "That's definitely a picture of Jeff Jennings and his parents."

"But he said his name was Randy," Lakshmi said.

Nan smiled gently at the young girl.

"Randy wasn't his real name, just a fake to make it harder to trace him."

"I don't understand," Mr. Manadhar said. "This Randy is such a fine young man. He spoke highly of his parents and talked about how he missed them, how proud he wanted to make them. He hardly spoke like a runaway who was angry at his parents!"

Mrs. Bobbsey shook her head. "Oh, we must find him. He only wanted a chance to grow up as he should."

Mrs. Manadhar spoke to her husband, who then addressed the Bobbseys. "My wife says she has been worried about him for some time. She says he has looked unwell, but she thinks it may be that he's very nervous. She saw fear in his eyes."

"Fear of what?" Mrs. Bobbsey asked.

Again Mr. Manadhar translated. "She does not know what caused the fear, only that she saw it in his eyes. Poor health perhaps, or financial problems. Who knows? She is anxious for us to find him, for she regards him almost as a son."

Freddie looked at Mohan. "You said that you and your sister went to his house. Can you show us?"

"Yeah, let's go!" Flossie added.

"I can drive you there," Mr. Manadhar offered. "I want to do whatever I can to help."

Mohan looked at his father. "Must we drive? It's a short walk to his house, and it's such a nice, warm night."

"I don't know," Mrs. Bobbsey said. "It's getting dark out."

"A walk would be fun!" Flossie said.

"I assure you that it's perfectly safe," Mr. Manadhar replied. "But I'm sure you'd prefer the convenience of a car."

"To be honest," Bert said, "it might scare Jeff if he saw all ten of us driving up to his house! Perhaps it would be better if we kids just walked down."

"Good point, Bert," Mr. Bobbsey agreed.

"Thanks, Dad," the four Bobbsey children said as they followed Mohan and Lakshmi out the door.

The Bobbseys gasped as they ran into the warm evening, for in the distance they saw the white peaks of the gigantic Himalayan mountains. The mountaintops stood out brightly in the darkening twilight.

But Mohan and Lakshmi had not stopped, for they were used to the sight of the tall, snowy mountains. "Hurry!" they shouted at their lingering guests.

They followed Lakshmi and Mohan down a narrow street. Men, women and children stood around, talking and visiting. Some of them stopped to stare, some of them to smile at the light-skinned Bobbseys.

"They don't seem upset that we're Americans," Nan commented.

"That's because you're children," Mohan said. "They'd still be suspicious of adults."

"Maybe that's why Jeff seemed nervous to Mrs. Manadhar," Bert said. "Perhaps he's scared that the Nepali will hate him because he's an American."

They neared a small, shabby white house, with a dim light shining through the dingy window in front. Bert stopped and stood near a large willow tree. "Maybe the four of us should wait here."

"Why?" Freddie asked.

"If he sees us," Bert said, "he may be too frightened to answer. I think we should talk to him, but let him at least answer the door, first."

"He won't be frightened of me!" Freddie said. "We're good buddies."

Meanwhile, Mohan and Lakshmi had continued walking across the lawn to the little house. They knocked at the door, but there was no answer.

The Bobbseys walked to the house to join their new friends.

"I guess it didn't matter who went," Flossie said sadly. "He wasn't there."

"My camera!" Freddie shouted. "We left so fast that I left it at the Manadhars' house."

"Don't worry," Nan said. "You'll get it when we go back."

"Maybe I could have used it for clues," Freddie said.

Flossie strained her neck to peek inside the window. "It's too tall for me!"

Nan and Bert came and looked into the window.

"Suppose someone sees us?" Lakshmi asked. "We could get into trouble."

"You're right," Mohan said. "Lakshmi, it's now your job to be our lookout!"

But Nan and Bert were dismayed by what they saw through the window. A thin cat howled miserably from behind the closed door. Broken dishes lay scattered on the floor, as if there had been a fight.

"What's this?" Flossie asked, picking up a piece of paper that lay in the dirt. "It has an address on it."

Mohan examined the dusty paper. "It's the address of the temple that was robbed two days ago!"

Later that night, Mr. Manadhar drove the Bobbseys through the dark, narrow streets to their hotel.

"It looks luxurious," Mrs. Bobbsey said,

as they arrived at the tall, modern building with bright lights twinkling from the many windows.

"It's the finest in the country," Mr. Manadhar said. "Enjoy your stay. I'll see you tomorrow."

"Thanks for dinner," Mrs. Bobbsey said. "We all enjoyed it very much."

"Our privilege," Mr. Manadhar said.

"It was great," Flossie said. "I hope your wife will give us the recipe so Dinah can learn to make it."

Mr. Bobbsey laughed. "If Dinah doesn't want to fix it, I'd sure be willing to!"

Mr. Manadhar looked startled. "You would cook it? Do men in your country do that?"

"Certainly," Mr. Bobbsey said, as his wife smiled happily. "Men in America often do as much housework as their wives, but many of the women also work outside the home."

Mr. Manadhar grinned. "I don't know if I should tell my wife about these customs!"

A bellboy carried the Bobbseys' luggage into the spacious lobby, which was lined with plush blue sofas and huge, green plants. Mr. Bobbsey went to the desk to check them in, while the family waited by the sofas.

Flossie pointed to an American man and woman getting out of the elevator and walking across the lobby. "Look! There's the man and woman from the airplane!"

"It is!" Nan exclaimed. "The ones sitting across from us."

"The ones who disappeared from the customs line," Bert added.

"I told you," Freddie said, "they didn't disappear. They dressed up as Nepali."

"Look at them," Flossie said. "They do look just like the Nay-plee couple we saw leaving the airport!"

"Yeah," Freddie added. "Anyway, how else would they have gotten out without us noticing?"

Mrs. Bobbsey looked at the couple. "You may be right. They certainly got out of the airport somehow. They do look a bit like the Nepali couple you pointed to."

Freddie took out his camera. "This time I'm getting a picture."

At that moment, a young, bearded man strode across the lobby to talk to the couple. As the man reached the couple, Freddie snapped the picture. The flash went off, causing a blaze of light that startled the three people. The surprised group turned and glared at the Bobbseys.

"We're sorry," Bert said. "It was an accident."

"Jeff!" Flossie shouted. "That's Jeff!"

But the young man with the beard had already hurried out of the hotel.

·5·
Clues in Kirtipur

After a good night's sleep and a hearty breakfast, the Bobbseys met Mr. Manadhar and Lakshmi and Mohan in the hotel lobby.

"*Namaste*," the Manadhars said. "Good morning."

"*Namaste*," the Bobbseys returned.

"I hope everyone is ready for sightseeing," Mr. Manadhar said. "It's a beautiful, warm day for it."

"Yes, we are," Mr. Bobbsey replied. "But how will all of us fit in your car?"

"Daddy rented a van!" Lakshmi squealed.

"Will Mrs. Manadhar be able to join us?" Mrs. Bobbsey asked.

"She has much to do today," Mr. Manadhar returned, "and begs to be excused. But tomorrow her day will be free. She would like the four of us to have lunch together then, after Richard and I have had our business meeting."

"Good," Mr. and Mrs. Bobbsey said. "That would be fun."

"And we kids can play together," Flossie said. "That would be fun!"

Freddie held out the picture he had taken in the lobby the night before. "Look! Here's a picture of our friend! Except now he has a beard."

"I wonder if Jeff recognized us," Flossie mused.

"We're not entirely sure it's Jeff," Mrs. Bobbsey said. "We haven't seen him since he grew his beard. It's more accurate to say that it *could* be Jeff."

The three Manadhars examined the

photograph. "That's definitely our friend Randy," Mohan said firmly.

"Yes," Lakshmi and her father agreed. "It's he."

"I wonder," said Mohan, "who the other two people are."

"Do you remember?" asked Nan. "At the airport yesterday, Flossie and Freddie said an American couple disappeared in the airport and didn't go through customs."

Mr. Manadhar stroked his chin. "Yes. But that would have been impossible."

"They dressed as Nay-pleese," Flossie said. "But these are the people we were talking about!"

"And they know Randy?" Lakshmi asked.

The Bobbseys explained how they had seen the people, and how Jeff had run away when Freddie snapped their picture.

"But we don't know any of the circumstances," Mrs. Bobbsey admitted.

"In that case," Mr. Manadhar said, "we should go back by Randy's—I mean, Jeff's—house and see if he's there. We can also drive to Kirtipur and see if the people at the university know anything about him."

Mohan looked at the younger Bobbseys. "Good! Kirtipur is—how do you say it?— neat!"

They drove the van past Jeff's house, but again, no one was home. This time, the Manadhars left a note asking him to please get in touch with them, for they missed him and were concerned.

The Bobbseys debated whether they, too, should leave a message. They decided not to. Right now, Jeff had no idea that the Manadhars and Bobbseys were friends. And the Bobbseys' surprise "meeting" with Jeff may have frightened him enough!

The cat was still inside, but sleeping. "We'll come back later," Mohan whispered to the other children, "and figure out a way to get food to the cat."

They rode four miles through the valley, surrounded by the mighty Himalayan mountains. They passed huts and cows and carefully tended fields, until they reached a large plateau. They drove up the plateau to Kirtipur.

"Wow!" Freddie exclaimed. "You can see the whole valley from here!"

Mr. Manadhar turned onto the narrow streets of the town. He blasted his horn. "I wish that cow would hurry and cross the road," he grumbled as he braked the van.

"Cat-pur's pretty," Flossie said as they passed beautifully carved temples and houses.

"It is," Mr. Manadhar agreed. "But Kirtipur has its share of poor homes, also."

They reached the modern university. They parked and walked until they reached the building marked "Administration," in both Nepali and English.

"*Namaste*," the dean told them as they entered his office. "What can I do for you?"

They inquired about their friend Randy Baker/Jeff Jennings. The dean phoned another office and spoke in Nepali, then returned to the Bobbseys and Manadhars.

"I am very sorry," the dean said in English, "but this young man has not been to any of his classes for the last three weeks. It is very sad, because I hear that he was one of our top students. But he will probably fail because of his unexplained, prolonged absence."

"Suppose he has a legitimate reason for being gone?" Bert asked. "Will he still fail?"

The dean shrugged. "Maybe. Maybe not. It depends on the reason. However, if he had a good reason, he would have gotten in touch with us. We see it all the time, good students dropping out, often just from boredom and laziness."

"He's not lazy!" Freddie insisted.

The dean gazed at the Manadhars and Bobbseys. "I have to be honest. It may be much worse than laziness. The police suspect he is involved with the recent thefts."

* * *

Mr. Manadhar drove them back into Kathmandu. "If you no longer feel like sightseeing, I understand."

"I think we should look around town," Mrs. Bobbsey said, forcing a smile. "Perhaps we can take our minds off Jeff's problems for a while."

They went to the Durbar Square, where the ancient kings of Kathmandu once had their palaces. The Manadhars led them through the crowds, past khaki-clad guards and tall Hindu temples. Freddie stopped to take pictures of every lovely building they came to.

"This is Kumari Ghar," Mr. Manadhar said, pointing to a pagoda-style building, "the house of the Living Goddess."

"What's that?" Flossie asked.

"She is a young girl," Mr. Manadhar explained, "especially chosen because we Hindus believe our goddess Kali actually lives in her."

"Look," Lakshmi said, pointing to a window, "there she is!"

An eight-year-old girl gazed out the window. Her large, dark, serious eyes were heavily lined with makeup, and she wore an elaborate headdress.

Freddie got out his camera, but Mr. Manadhar shook his head. "Taking her picture is not allowed."

"It must be great being a living goddess!" Flossie exclaimed. She pictured herself at the window, staring down at the crowds who came to gawk at her and offer her their respect.

"She hardly ever leaves her home," Lakshmi said. "And she is carried places, because she's not supposed to walk. When she grows up, she can never marry. I'm glad that I'm no living goddess!"

"There's no chance of that!" Mohan laughed. "But it does have its good points. Even the king worships her."

Flossie looked back up at the little girl and then at Lakshmi. "Maybe it is better this way!"

A few yards away, a woman in a ragged

sari banged on a temple door, shouting loudly in Nepali.

"She begs to be let into the temple," Mr. Manadhar said solemnly.

"Why can't she go in?" Nan asked.

"The recent thefts," Mr. Manadhar replied. "Many of the temples are locked now, because of the ones that have been looted."

Bert looked around at the crowds moving past. "They don't look very friendly," he muttered.

"I am so sorry," Mr. Manadhar said. "It seems the situation is getting worse, especially since Americans are blamed for the thefts. The people are frightened. They say the gods have no power if the temple's treasures can be stolen. If they have no power, the gods cannot protect the people. The thieves must be found, so the people will not be so afraid!"

"We'll do our best to help," Freddie said.

Mr. Manadhar patted him on the head. "I appreciate the offer, but what can children do?" he asked, as the Bobbseys smiled knowingly at each other.

The woman banged her shoe on the temple door, and she wailed louder and louder and wept.

"She screams that we must get our statues back," Mr. Manadhar said. "If not, she says we all will die!"

·6·

The Jeweled Buddhas

Flossie clutched the small package of meat as the Bobbseys walked with Mohan and Lakshmi. "I hope the cat likes this."

Nan smiled. "Of course he will. Anyway, the poor thing looked hungry enough to eat anything!"

The mid-afternoon sun blazed overhead as Mohan spoke. "Mother said that she'd fix dinner later than usual. That way we could play. She didn't know that she gave us time to take care of Randy's cat."

"I'm just glad," Lakshmi giggled, "that I didn't have to stay and help cook!"

"I hope that we don't have any trouble getting into Jeff's house," Bert remarked.

Nan nodded. "I know, but what choice do we have? The poor animal looked starved. He doesn't look well cared for."

"Something bad must have happened," Freddie said. "Jeff takes good care of animals!"

"Not this one," Bert said sadly, as the group of six neared the small house.

They glanced around to make sure no one was watching. To their relief, only three people were out on the street, and they were too busy with their own chores to pay attention to the children.

They knocked on the door in case Jeff had finally come home. There was no answer, only the cat's pitiful meow. However, the Manadhars' note to Jeff was no longer there.

Nan and Bert looked in through the front window. The broken dishes still lay on the floor. Nothing had changed since the day before.

"How will we get in?" Flossie asked while turning the door handle. To her surprise, it opened!

They entered the dusty house and locked the door behind them. The kitten ran eagerly toward them.

"Should we clean up the dishes?" Mohan asked.

"No," said Freddie. "They could be a clue."

Mohan looked puzzled. "How?"

"They could have been thrown down during a fight," Bert explained, "or thrown on purpose. Since we don't know why they're down there, we should leave them, at least until we do know."

"He wouldn't do something like that on purpose," Lakshmi said.

Flossie looked thoughtful. "Unless he's trying to fool someone."

"At any rate," Nan said, "we're hardly

invited guests. He might not appreciate our cleaning up!"

Nan found a dish and Flossie put the meat on it. They set it on the floor, but the cat only picked at it. The animal was more eager to purr and play with the children.

They looked nervously at each other, for suddenly they heard voices outside. Men were talking to each other and coming closer to the house!

The children scrambled into the other room and crouched by the bed. As Flossie knelt down, she noticed a tiny dish of cat food in the corner. The cat had food, after all!

"Randy!" a man yelled from the front, pounding on the door. "If you're in there, come out!"

"We need to talk to you," another man said.

"He's not here, boss!" the first man said, looking through the window and seeing only the cat. Someone slipped a note under the door, then they walked away.

The children crept back into the other room when they heard the footsteps fade away. They glanced through the window. There were three American men. Two were tall and dark-headed, and the third was short and balding. The children could only see the backs of their heads, but one of the men turned around and faced the house.

"He's ugly," Flossie whispered when she saw him. Indeed, a hideous scar ran down the side of his face, and his eyes were grim and mean.

"Did you hear something, boss?" the man said, turning back around.

"Nah," the short man said. "No one's there. Let's go. We'll find him later." They got in a dark blue car and left.

Freddie picked up the note that had been slipped underneath the door. "Randy," it said, "please contact us. We need you for another chauffeuring job. Meet us at the temple. You know which one."

The next morning after breakfast, the Manadhar and Bobbsey children went back out walking. "I wonder if your father was right," Bert said.

Mohan shrugged. "I do not know. But he seemed very convinced that we should stay out of Randy's problems."

"He thinks it's dangerous," Lakshmi added.

Freddie stuck out his lip. "It may be, but we're not afraid. We have to help our friend."

"I'm afraid," Lakshmi said timidly. "But I'll still help if I can."

They stopped walking, for they saw a woman chasing a boar out of her house.

"Get out!" she yelled, swatting the animal with a broom.

Freddie got his camera out and took a picture. The woman looked up and laughed with the children. Then she went back inside. The boar followed her in.

The children continued walking, laughing as the woman shrieked at the boar!

They turned onto another narrow street and walked past a row of open-air stalls. Some had food hanging on string from the ceiling, while others had pots and jugs and saris. They walked slowly so the Bobbseys could look at the many shops lining the road.

A young boy with serious, black eyes and dressed in dark red robes, waved to the children, then pressed his hands together in front of his face. "Mohan, Lakshmi. *Namaste.*"

"Dorje!" the Manadhar children shouted. "It's good to see you. Come meet our American friends."

And Dorje ran toward the children and burst into tears. "They stole Lord Buddha!" he cried. "Our temple has just been robbed!"

·7·

A Buddhist Temple

Mohan blinked in astonishment. "What? Another robbery?"

"Yes," Dorje sobbed. "By our own monks!"

"Tell us what happened," Nan urged.

Dorje dried his eyes with the corner of his robe. "I was in the temple, dusting the books and altars, when I heard strange noises. I hid, and then I saw three men— monks. They took the two small statues of the Buddha, tucked them under their robes, and ran out."

Flossie's eyes grew wide. "You mean monkeys stole the statue? I can't believe it!"

"No, Flossie," Bert said. "Monk-*eys* are animals in zoos. Monks dedicate themselves to religion. A slight difference!"

"Dorje himself is a monk," Mohan said proudly, introducing him to the four Bobbseys. "A Buddhist monk."

Dorje hung his head. "I am not very proud of my monastery now. The thieves are from there, too. Can you imagine? The sacrilege was committed by people I live with, study with, and pray with!"

"We're walking to Syambanoth," Mohan said. "Would you like to join us and tell us about it?"

"Ah, the monkey temple," Dorje replied. "Thank you. I'd like that."

"Monkey temple?" Flossie asked, confused.

Lakshmi giggled. "There are lots of monkeys there!"

"I'd like to see *your* temple," Flossie said to Dorje. "You're the first monk I ever met."

"Good idea!" Nan said. "Maybe there are clues. Is it far from here?"

Dorje shook his head. "No, it is not far at all. It is practically on the way to Syamba-noth."

The group of seven walked down the dusty, narrow street. A cart, pulled by oxen, rumbled through. The children laughed, because a car pulled up behind the cart. The automobile driver was impatient, for the cart was very slow, and he honked and yelled at the man and oxen holding him up.

The driver of the cart simply turned toward the car, talked in Nepali, laughed, then continued as before. The driver yelled back, but the man driving the oxen did not flinch or hurry the beasts.

"What did he say?" Freddie asked, taking a photograph of the unusual traffic jam.

Mohan laughed. "He said that perhaps the other man would learn better patience if he got himself some oxen!"

The oxen cart plodded on, and the car still crept behind it. The street was too narrow for the driver to get around the oxen.

"Did you say you lived at the monastery?" Freddie asked. "Can we meet your parents when we get there?"

"They do not live there," Dorje said. "They live at home with my sisters and brothers."

"Don't you miss them?" Flossie asked. "It must be awful to be separated like that!"

"Sometimes I miss them," he replied, "but I'm happy in the monastery. I often get to see my family, but now the other monks are my family. That's why the theft makes me so ashamed."

"Did the police have any ideas?" Bert asked as they turned a corner onto another street.

Dorje shrugged. "They are investigating all who live at our monastery. They're confused, for they say it's different from the other crimes. The others are believed to have been committed by Americans."

"Maybe the monks thought they could get away with it," Freddie said, "if they thought others would be blamed."

"I'm afraid you're probably right," Dorje said sadly as they neared a large white building. "There's the temple. At least the police seem to have gone away."

They walked to the temple doorway, and Dorje told the others to take off their shoes and leave them on the porch. Then they silently entered.

"It's bee-yoo-ti-ful," Flossie whispered as she gazed at the huge, golden statue of the Buddha. The room was full of candles, and incense perfumed the air. Smaller gold statues were placed around the room.

"What did they take?" Flossie asked. "There are so many stat-chutes here now."

"They stole the two statues with the jewels," Dorje replied. "They were the most valuable statues we had, and the most ancient. According to legend, they are almost two thousand years old! They are said to have been brought to Nepal from India by Ashoka, a great Indian king of ancient days."

"Not those!" Lakshmi exclaimed. "Not the jeweled statues!"

"Yes, I'm afraid so," Dorje said, turning toward the Bobbseys to explain. "You see, the statues have many jewels on them. They are gold and have a large diamond in the forehead, rubies around the lips, and sapphires for the eyes."

"Sounds lovely," Flossie whispered.

"And worth a fortune!" Bert whistled.

"They are priceless," Dorje said, "though the worth of such a thing cannot be measured in money."

"Where were the statues kept before they were stolen?" Bert asked.

Dorje pointed to bare spots on both sides of the altar. "One stood on each side, right here."

Flossie glimpsed a bit of silver shining underneath the altar. She knelt down for a better look. A silver necklace, with a picture

of the Buddha surrounded by lotus blossoms, lay in the dust on the floor.

She picked it up with a Kleenex and held it out for the others to see. "Look what I found!"

"I wonder if the thieves could have dropped it," Freddie said.

Dorje shuffled his feet, then showed them his own necklace, identical to the one Flossie had found. "This is worn by all the monks in our monastery. No one else in the entire world wears such a necklace."

"Did you get a good enough look at the thieves," Nan said, "to recognize them?"

"I saw their faces," Dorje said, "but I did not recognize them. However, there are many monks at our monastery, and sometimes new ones come and old ones go. It is hard to know everyone."

"Tell us what they look like," Freddie urged.

"Well," Dorje replied, "their hair was very black and shiny, but clipped short like mine. They had red robes like mine—and necklaces like mine. Two of the men were tall, much taller than most Nepali. One was shorter. The other monks seemed angry with him, though, because he blew his nose very loudly."

Flossie looked up. "He blew his nose loud?"

Dorje nodded. "It sounded like a goose honking. I never heard anything like it before!"

Just then an older monk walked in and patted Dorje on the shoulder. "This is a sad day for us, my boy."

"Yes, Rinpoche," Dorje said. He then introduced the Bobbseys and Manadhars to his teacher.

"*Namaste*. It is nice to meet you," Rinpoche said, shaking the Bobbseys' hands in the American fashion. "I am sorry for you to come to our temple on such a shameful day."

"We do a lot of detective work at home," Freddie said. "We'd be happy to help any way we can."

"Thank you," Rinpoche said. "As it is, the police are questioning all of us. There's something that doesn't make sense, though."

"What's that?" Flossie asked.

Rinpoche wrinkled his bushy eyebrows. "A young American man with a beard drove the car the monks escaped in."

"An American!" Nan exclaimed. "Did anyone get a good look at him?"

"I did," Rinpoche replied. "I was standing outside, before I even knew we had been robbed. I was giving food to some of the poor people in the neighborhood, when I noticed a young American man waiting in a car. Suddenly, three monks hurried out, and the young man got out to open the car door for them. Then he drove them away. After I found out about the robbery, I described him to the police. They think his name is Randy Baker."

"Oh, goodness," Nan murmured. "It sounds like Jeff really has become a thief!"

"Of course he's not," Freddie snapped.

"There are probably lots of Americans here."

"I know," Nan said. "But he is a student in Kirtipur. And remember those men who came looking for him yesterday? And the note they left about the temple? You must admit, it looks suspicious."

Freddie shrugged. "So what? It only means that it's real important for us to find the real thieves! Jeff's my friend, and he's not a thief!"

"I sure hope you're right," Nan said wistfully. "But it sounds like he *is* a thief!"

·8·

Monkeys and Monks

Flossie put her hands on her hips and looked at her twin brother. "Don't worry, Freddie. We'll solve this case and prove he's innocent."

"I hope we're wrong," Bert said. "We'll just have to find the thieves and get to the bottom of this!"

"I wonder," Freddie said, "if the thieves weren't really monks. Maybe they just dressed up like monks."

Dorje scratched his head. "How? They had on the necklace."

"I would be very grateful," Rinpoche said, "if we discovered that at least our own monks didn't steal the statues!"

"Could they have gotten the necklaces somehow?" Bert asked. "Where do your people get the necklaces?"

"There is a silversmith nearby," Rinpoche said, "and he makes them. Dorje knows the place."

"Let's talk to him," Flossie said. "Dorje, would you show us?"

"I'd be happy to," Dorje replied. "It's very close by."

"I thought you said it wasn't far," Flossie said, panting as the group reached the top of a steep hill.

"It's not," Dorje smiled. "This was only four kilometers from the temple."

"All uphill!" Freddie said. "Why don't we rest for a minute. For Flossie's sake, of course. *I'm* not tired."

They sat by the roadside on the hilltop. Freddie got out his camera and photographed the homes and shops at which they were looking down.

Mohan noticed a fruit stall behind them. "I'll be back in a minute," he said, getting up.

He soon returned with a bunch of bananas for all the children to share. While they rested, they snacked.

Flossie sat for a moment, holding her banana, when suddenly it was no longer in her hand. "Freddie, why'd you do that?" she shouted.

"Do what?" he asked.

"You took my banana," she snapped. "Give it back."

"I don't have your dumb banana," he said.

"I think I see the culprit," Nan said, pointing to a monkey that sat behind Flossie, eating her banana!

They all laughed, and Flossie apologized to Freddie. Then the monkey wiped his mouth with his hand, reached over, and grabbed Freddie's banana!

Soon they got back up and Dorje led them down a winding street to the silversmith's shop. A small Nepali man greeted them.

Dorje explained to Mr. Kumar about the necklace they had found at the robbery. "Did you make any for anyone outside the monastery?" he asked.

Mr. Kumar scratched his chin. "No, just for those new monks," he said in English. "I hate to say this, but those new monks seemed a bit odd."

"Odd?" Flossie repeated. "How?"

Mr. Kumar sat cross-legged on the floor. "Well," he continued, "I don't usually make the necklaces for the monks, themselves. It's unusual to have them come directly to me."

Dorje turned to the Manadhars and Bobbseys. "Usually, one person from the monastery comes to Mr. Kumar for the order. That person distributes the necklaces to the monks."

Mr. Kumar grinned. "And that one person is usually my young friend Dorje! But these monks said they had lost their necklaces. I asked them how, since they're never supposed to take them off. But it seems they had gotten tangled somehow in jungle brush. I agreed to make their necklaces. They asked me not to tell anyone, because they were afraid the abbot would be angry at their carelessness. Is that why you wanted to know this? Did Rinpoche find out and get angry after all?"

"The temple was robbed," Bert explained. "The thieves were dressed as monks. The men who came to you might have been the thieves."

Mr. Kumar's hand flew to his mouth. "Oh, no! Is that why they wanted my necklaces? To rob the temple? And I'm to blame!"

"No, no, Mr. Kumar," Nan said. "It's hardly your fault. But you must tell us if there's anything else you remember."

"Just one thing," Mr. Kumar said. "A lady

was waiting outside for them. She was very attractive and tall, with dark hair and stylish clothes. I thought it odd that monks should have a woman waiting!"

Freddie pulled his snapshot of Jeff and the American couple from his pocket. "Could this be the woman?" he asked.

"Why, yes," Mr. Kumar replied. "She does look familiar. And so does this man."

"The older man, right?" Freddie said.

Mr. Kumar shook his head. "No, the younger one. He is the one who picked up the necklace order to deliver to the monks!"

"That's Jeff's picture, all right," Bert said, sorry to have his friend positively identified as one of the thieves.

·9·

The Sacred
Syambanoth Shrine

"No!" Freddie shouted. "I don't believe it."

Flossie scratched her chin. "'Member those men who were looking for Jeff at his house? Maybe they're all tied together in this."

"No," Freddie insisted. "Jeff's not tied up in this!"

Bert laid his hand on his brother's shoulder. "I know how you feel. None of us wants to see an old friend in trouble. Why don't we all go on to the monkey temple? I think we could all use some cheering up."

"Ah, yes," Mr. Kumar said. "That's a good place to see. Why, the building is at least two thousand years old."

"Yes," Lakshmi giggled. "It's also fun seeing the monkeys. There are so many there! They seem to like Syambanoth a lot, though no one knows why—the monkeys won't tell us!"

Mr. Kumar nodded. "You'll also have a chance to see the new statue that a Thai monk gave the temple there. I hear it is jade—a small, but exact, replica of the so-called Emerald Buddha in Bangkok. Very valuable!"

"A new, valuable statue?" Freddie murmured. "Sounds like a good place for the thieves to strike."

Mr. Kumar shook his head. "I hope not. But I can't imagine that even criminal monks would have the nerve to rob Syambanoth. It's one of the most sacred Buddhist shrines in the world!"

"Unless they were fake monks," Flossie said.

"Anyway," Nan said, "I'd hate to take the chance of another robbery."

"This is a very sad day," Mr. Kumar said, hanging his head. "Imagine! Monks stealing from temples, and holy places in danger!"

"Don't worry," Bert said. "We'll find the culprits. We're pretty good detectives."

Mr. Kumar brightened and held out his hand. "I believe you *will* solve the case. We will all be very grateful. Here. Before you go, I want the Bobbseys to have some presents to help them remember Nepal. It is my way of thanking you for helping." He handed Nan and Flossie dainty silver earrings, and the boys each got a silver-handled pocketknife.

"But you don't have to give us anything," the Bobbseys protested at once. "We like helping."

"Please," Mr. Kumar said. "I want you to have these things. Just think—my silver pieces in America!"

"Then thank you," they squealed, putting their new treasures in their pockets.

The children walked back down the hill along the narrow road. They turned onto an even narrower road that took them past small homes with flowering potted plants in the windows and on front porches.

"Are we close?" Flossie asked, panting, after they had walked another mile.

"Yes," Lakshmi said, pointing ahead. "There's Syambanoth."

A steep hill, topped by a tall, golden spire painted with a pair of eyes on each side, loomed in front of them.

"We have to climb the steps to get there," Mohan said. "I believe there are over three hundred of them."

"Oh, well," Flossie said, "I guess we'll have strong leg muscles from all this walking!"

The area was noisy, but they looked up, startled, when they heard a man loudly blowing his nose. The children looked around, but saw no one familiar.

They climbed the long staircase, which was crowded with scampering monkeys, tourists, beggars, and pious folk just coming to pray. They stopped to rest at a landing lined with vendors' tables. Nan stopped to buy a Nepali doll in a sari to add to her growing collection.

Finally they reached the top. The tall, golden spire, with a domed base, stood in the center. It was surrounded by small temples the size of sheds, and shrines. A large temple, snack bar, and library stood to one side. The area was crowded with people and monkeys. One policeman walked around examining the crowd and watching the temple doors.

"What are these?" Freddie asked, pointing to large, red cylinders standing near a shrine.

"They're prayer wheels," Dorje said as an old woman walked up to the prayer wheels. "Our people believe that we spin these and send our prayers to all the earth. Written prayers are inside the wheels."

"Look!" Flossie giggled. "The monkey's praying." A monkey had scampered up to the area, next to the old woman. Side by side, the monkey and the lady ignored each other while serenely spinning the wheels!

"I suspect," Freddie said, while snapping a picture of the unusual couple, "that if we keep our eyes open, we'll see our old friend from the plane."

"Because we heard someone blowing his nose?" Bert asked. "Lots of people blow their noses."

They walked past the lone policeman and entered the temple. A small statue, bright green, sat behind the altar, high on a shelf, by a giant-sized statue of the Buddha.

"Gosh!" Freddie breathed. "That's something else!"

A Nepali couple stood off to the side. The man talked in a low voice to a tall, dark-skinned woman, dressed in a sari, who gazed at the new statue and scribbled on a notepad.

"Odd," Bert said. "They're Nepali, yet she told him in English to be quiet."

"They're the people from the plane," Flossie said.

They all grew quiet, pretending to be admiring the statue, while they strained their ears to listen to the others' conversation.

"We'll meet Randy and the others here in two hours," they heard her say. "After that, the statue will be ours!"

·10·

A Talk with Police

Freddie glanced at the couple. The woman, suddenly aware that they were being watched, grew silent and stopped writing. She and the man smiled nonchalantly at the children, said *"namaste,"* and hurried from the temple.

"I bet those were the Americans we saw on the airplane," Flossie said.

"Quite possibly," Nan said. "But we can't really be sure."

"We should tell the police," Bert said as they walked thoughtfully out of the temple and down the long staircase.

"I'll show you the way," Mohan said.

They followed Mohan down a dusty, winding road for a short distance. They reached a square, white building with khaki-clad men chatting in front. The men smiled and nodded as the children walked in.

They entered a room full of desks and policemen. They were directed toward a tall, uniformed man who spoke no English. Mohan translated for the Bobbseys. "We want to report a robbery," he said.

The officer jerked his head and put his hand on his holster. "Where?"

"It hasn't happened yet," Mohan explained. "A man and woman were at Syambanoth, and we heard them say they planned to rob the temple in two hours."

"Ah," the man said, his lips curving into a smile. "You heard someone say this. Who? Your friends here?" He laughed and waved his arms in the direction of the other children.

Dorje spoke up. "No! We heard two grown-ups say this. A Nepali man and woman. Or rather they looked like Nepali. They could have been Americans that the Bobbseys know." He pointed in the direction of his new friends.

The man put his hands on his hips. "Americans who look like Nepali? That's what you and your little friends think? Don't waste my time!"

Flossie noticed that a young policeman was watching them with interest. He moved close enough to overhear the conversation. She hoped he, at least, believed them. It was obvious by now that the man they were talking to now certainly didn't!

"Can't you tell him we're detectives?" Nan whispered.

Mohan told this to the officer, who only shook his head. "Look," he said. "I have no time for childish games. No Nepali would rob Syambanoth, as holy as it is! Go away. We have important things to do. We must find the *real* criminals! Why, we have even identified one of them."

"You have?" Mohan asked. "Who?"

"A young American," the officer growled. "Perhaps the criminal is the kind that *your* friends would know. No matter. We'll catch him soon. Now go!" He shooed them away.

Mohan translated the fruitless conversation to the Bobbseys as they left the police station.

"Now it's up to us to prevent a robbery!" Bert said.

"And help our friend," Freddie added.

"Let's walk to Jeff's house," Nan suggested.

They headed back toward the little white house. Perhaps they could find Jeff there. Since the cat had been fed the day before, they knew that he sometimes went to his house. If they could only talk to Jeff and find out the truth!

"Gosh," Flossie said as they walked, "I just realized I'm not tired from walking anymore!"

"We're getting used to it," Nan smiled. "We'll certainly go home in good physical shape!"

When they were within a half-mile of the house, they saw a car drive toward Jeff's house. It was the same dark blue car they had seen there before. They glanced inside the car at the passengers—and saw the tall man's scar on the side of his face!

They hung back so they wouldn't be noticed, and watched and followed. Luckily, the car had to drive slowly, for cows and children wandered freely in the narrow street. But the children still had to trot to keep up! After a few minutes, however, the men pulled over and stopped at a food stall.

The panting children drew near and crouched behind bushes as one of the men munched on chapatis and curry, and talked.

"I wonder where Randy has gone now!" the man with the scar said.

"He's a coward if you ask me," his friend replied. "I'm getting tired of looking all over town every time we need him for a job. Hurry and eat. We don't have time to waste."

"But I'm hungry. Don't worry. We'll find him," the first one said. "I'm not about to go back to the boss and tell him that Randy's disappeared. Then *we'll* be the ones in trouble. No sir. Randy's going to be found, and he'll regret every time he's been a nuisance to us."

"Well, let's get on to his house," the man replied. "He'd better be there, this time."

"One thing's been great," the other said. "Randy's the only one the cops have even been able to identify. They're so busy looking for him that they haven't any idea about the rest of us."

"Yeah," his chum answered. "We'd better just get to Randy before the cops do!

And when we do . . . like I said, he'll be sorry!"

Freddie's eyes grew wide. "And *we* have to find Jeff before everyone else," he whispered.

·11·

Reunion with a Friend

"We'd better hurry and get to Jeff's house," Nan said. "I wish there was a way to get there before them."

"There is," Mohan answered. "I'll show you a shortcut."

Mohan and Lakshmi led the children as they ran through a narrow alley behind houses, between homes, even cutting through a woman's yard. A woman yelled in Nepali, but they ran so fast, they didn't hear her or her barking dog.

Finally, the panting children came upon Jeff's white house from behind. Sure enough, the men had just arrived.

The Bobbseys hid, for Americans were sure to attract attention. Dorje, Lakshmi, and Mohan wandered nonchalantly in front, acting as if they paid no attention to the little house. However, they listened intently and watched Jeff's house from the corner of their eyes. And the Bobbseys, hidden behind the house, listened breathlessly, wishing they could see, hoping Jeff wouldn't be there for the men to find! But if he was, they were ready to help!

The men banged on the door, but no one answered. They finally pushed it open and went in. The three Nepali children sat in the yard, as if they were playing a game.

Within seconds the men re-emerged. "Where could he be?" one hollered. "It doesn't look like he's been home for weeks!" They got back in the car, gunned the engine, and left.

The Bobbseys came out from hiding and

joined their friends. "If I were Jeff," Bert said, "I'd be in a place the thugs would never think of." He turned to Freddie. "You were closer to him than the rest of us. What do you think?"

Freddie shut his eyes and thought for a moment. "I know!" he shouted. "There are two things Jeff loved more than anything. One's soccer. He's taught me a lot about soccer. He's really good, and he loves to watch. And reading is the other. At home, the library was one of his favorite places to go."

"The library!" Bert exclaimed. "He could easily be hiding there. The thugs would never think to look there, I'll bet!"

Freddie lit up. "Let's go there and look!"

"Shouldn't we also keep an eye on the monk temple?" Flossie suggested.

"Yes," Nan said. "Maybe we could split up. And I think we need to call Mom and Dad and let them know what's going on!"

"If we can find a working telephone!" Mohan added.

"I thought Mummy and Daddy," Lakshmi said, "were taking Mr. and Mrs. Bobbsey for a drive in the mountains today. At least, after our fathers meet over their lumber business."

"That's right," Flossie groaned. "By the time they get back, the temple will have been robbed!"

"Unless we prevent it!" Bert said, eyeing his companions. "Mohan, Flossie, and I will go to the temple. Lakshmi, can you show Freddie, Nan, and Dorje where the library is?"

Nan quickly wrote a note to Jeff, just in case he did come back, and slipped it under the door. It warned him of danger and offered their help.

"We don't want to attract too much 'tension," Flossie said as the others took off for the library. "I have an idea."

Soon Flossie's and Bert's faces and hands were stained dark with walnut. They bought native clothing cheaply at a stand. Flossie wore a crudely draped sari and Bert had on baggy cotton slacks and a loose cotton shirt, just like Mohan's. He even wore the Nepali cap. They even smeared mud on their hair and on their faces and hands, and Flossie hid her blond curls underneath a long scarf.

"You look like beggars!" Mohan laughed, as they hid their other clothes and their shoes underneath a large stone before hurrying to Syambanoth. "No one would recognize you now!"

Nan, Lakshmi, and Freddie turned a corner and entered an old, three-story, stone building. The floors were dusty and creaked as they walked, but there was scarcely any other sound.

Freddie's heart thumped, for he was anxious to find his old friend, and frightened, too. It looked bad. Suppose Jeff really was in with the crooks? No, he refused to believe it. Jeff would have an explanation.

The librarian, a middle-aged Nepali man,

smiled when he saw Lakshmi. "*Namaste.*
You've come for more books?" he whispered.

She shook her head. "We're looking for
our friend Randy."

"I haven't seen him," the librarian said.
"But you're welcome to look around."

They crept past tall shelves full of books.
Most of them were written in the Nepali
language, which the Bobbseys could not
translate, but some were in English. People
sat around the tables, reading silently. The
children walked past and looked at the read-
ers. No one was familiar.

They climbed the stairs to the second
floor, looking again, but still with no luck.
Dejected, they went to the third. They
looked at all the people. No sign of Jeff.

Freddie shrugged, then turned around.
That man, sitting off in the corner, reading
where the light was very poor. Something
seemed familiar about him. It didn't look
like Jeff. The man in the corner was a
Nepali, with gray hair. But . . .

Freddie tiptoed over for another look. He stared at the man, whose face was practically buried in a huge book. The man coughed and looked up and his blue eyes met Freddie's.

"Jeff!" Freddie whispered. "It *is* you! We've been looking all over for you!"

Jeff's mouth dropped open in surprise. "Freddie Bobbsey! And Nan and Lakshmi! How on earth? That *was* you I saw at the hotel!"

"We want to help you," Nan said quietly.

Jeff hid his face in his hands. "I don't know if anyone can help me," he whispered harshly. "I'm in mighty bad trouble!"

·12·

Culprits in the Temple

Mohan, Flossie, and Bert easily climbed the long staircase to the temple. Their exhaustion from all their walking had vanished. They were too concerned about the impending robbery to think of anything else.

People swarmed around them, on their way to and from the temple, but this time there were no stares. No one would have guessed that any of these children were foreigners!

"There are so many people here," Bert

remarked as they reached the top. "It could make it easy for the thieves to grab the statue and get away."

They poked their heads inside the main temple, where the unguarded statue sat on the altar. The place was empty, except for an elderly monk, who looked too old and feeble to be one of the thieves from the previous robbery.

"Let's go outside and look," Flossie suggested.

The children spread out and wandered around the central tower painted with the huge eyes. A little girl ran up to Flossie, pointed at her face, and muttered in Nepali. Flossie blankly returned her gaze. After all, just because she looked like a Nepali didn't help her to understand the language!

Mohan saw the exchange from a distance. He laughed and approached Flossie's new friend. He spoke to the girl in Nepali, who turned and left.

"What was that all about?" Flossie asked.

Mohan smiled. "She's never seen blue eyes before. I told her that you were from a distant region, and that your dialect was different from hers. I explained that you couldn't understand her."

"Well," Flossie giggled. "I *am* from a distant region, and my diet-leg sure is different!" Her face turned serious. "Did you have any luck?"

He shrugged. "No. I didn't see those people anywhere."

They headed back toward the temple, where they met Bert.

"I didn't see anyone either," Bert reported. "Maybe there won't be a robbery after all."

Just then, Flossie looked around. "Ooo-eee," she squealed. "Look!"

On the other side they saw four people, dressed as Nepali, who were slowly advancing toward the temple. One of the men had a long scar on the side of his face. And the children again saw the man and woman they had seen taking notes at the temple!

The woman carried a basket filled with fruit and draped with a blanket. She smiled and chattered to the three men with her.

Flossie wound her way through the crowd, moving close enough to overhear the woman's conversation.

"I don't care how hard you looked," the woman said, through a false smile. "I'm very upset you didn't find him. You two will pay for this, I swear. But we'll worry about that later. Right now, we'll just concentrate on the newest addition to our growing collection of statues!"

Flossie ran back to her friends with her new information. Meanwhile, the four thieves moved steadily toward the temple. The children anxiously looked around for the guard, but he had disappeared from sight.

"I'm scared," Flossie whispered. "How can three of us handle four gangsters?"

Dorje, Lakshmi, Freddie, and Nan hurried out of the library. They turned and waved good-bye to Jeff, who was heading toward the nearby police station. He had agreed to turn himself in.

"I know you can prove you're innocent!" Freddie shouted to his good friend.

The children practically ran down the winding streets to reach Syambanoth. There wasn't much time. They expected the thieves any minute now!

Three Nepali children approached the little group who moved briskly along. "Candy?" they asked, stretching out their hands.

"Many of the children here seem to expect Americans to have candy for them," Dorje explained.

A little hand tugged at the camera bag hanging from Freddie's shoulder. "Photo?" a little voice asked. "Photo?"

"Later," Freddie muttered, trying to get around the children.

Two more Nepali children came to see if their friends were having success wheedling candy and pictures from the Americans. More hands reached toward the Bobbseys.

"Move!" Lakshmi shouted in Nepali. "They have nothing for you."

"Wait, Lakshmi," Freddie said. "Tell them to follow us. If they will, Nan and I will give them candy later and take everyone's picture! And Lakshmi—shout that to children all along the way."

Lakshmi was puzzled, but did as she was told. More and more children hurried from their homes to join the group.

Nan laughed. "I get it. We're taking a children's army with us!"

Within minutes they were at Syamba-noth, and a mob of children, still shouting for candy and photos, rushed up the stair-case. Lakshmi and Dorje had become sepa-rated from Nan and Freddie, but they all charged ahead.

The Bobbseys scanned the people at the top. They didn't see the thieves, but they didn't see Mohan, Flossie, and Bert, either!

They headed into the large temple. Fred-die and Nan gasped. The statue was gone! A pile of fruit sat where the statue had been!

The temple was now full of children, but Freddie thought he heard a muffled "ooo-eee" coming from the back of the temple. From the middle of the crowd, Lakshmi and Dorje shouted in Nepali, "The temple's been robbed!"

They all ran toward the back and into a small room just off the main building. The two big men were holding and trying to tie up the squirming children.

"Nosy brats!" the man with the scar shouted. "We'll teach you to meddle!"

The woman laughed and the other man

blew his nose loudly and told his companions to hurry. Then they all noticed the horde of children pressing in.

The crooks looked up startled as children swarmed into the small room. The woman grabbed her basket, and the four tried to leave, but they couldn't push past the children surrounding them.

Flossie, Bert, and Mohan wrestled themselves loose, for the thugs were more concerned with trying to escape. The woman held tightly to her basket. Nan and Bert, guessing that the basket contained the priceless statue, pulled at it with all their might. The shorter man tried to help her, but Freddie pitched in and the Bobbseys won the tug-of-war.

The crooks yelled and tried to push against the children, but to no avail. Everywhere they moved, children shoved against them.

Just as the Bobbseys began to worry that the stalemate wouldn't last long enough to prevent the crooks' escape, a whistle shrieked above the din. It was the young policeman who had watched the Bobbseys at the police station. The man squeezed through the children and arrested the four thieves. He handcuffed them, while the children helped hold them against the wall.

"You believed us after all!" Flossie said.

He spoke Nepali into his walkie-talkie, then looked back at the Bobbseys. "Yes," he said in English. "You seemed sincere. And when I turn in these worms, the rest of my colleagues will believe you! They should be here soon to take these people away, and I imagine that they'll be very grateful to you, as I am."

Nan smiled. "Thank you. We were just glad to stop the robberies."

"Could I ask you a favor?" Bert said to the policeman. "Could you radio back in and ask them to phone our parents?"

"Yes, I'd be happy to," the policeman answered.

"If anyone reaches them," Freddie asked, "could they give them a message for me? Would someone tell them that Jeff is in jail? And would someone tell them that I need a thousand pieces of candy and lots of film?"

·13·

Homeward Bound

Two police cars delivered the seven tired children to the Manadhars' home. The Manadhars and Bobbseys ran outside to greet and hug the children.

"We're so proud of you—again!" Mrs. Bobbsey said.

"We couldn't have done it without Lakshmi, Mohan, and Dorje!" Flossie bubbled as the Manadhars beamed.

"The police department was really nice,"

Bert said. "They gave candy to everyone in our children's army."

Mr. Bobbsey patted Freddie on the shoulder. "I understand that your army will regroup tomorrow for one big photography session. You'll certainly get lots of practice with that camera!"

Freddie hung his head. "I'm, glad we caught the thieves. I'm just sad about Jeff."

"I understand," Mr. Bobbsey replied. "Why don't you come on inside and rest? You kids must be exhausted."

The children walked in and gasped in surprise. A smiling Jeff and his parents were waiting inside the house!

"We cabled Mr. and Mrs. Jennings," Mrs. Bobbsey explained, "as soon as we knew that Jeff was in town. Of course, we hadn't exactly found him, but we knew you children would locate him!"

"And my wife felt better the minute we heard from the Bobbseys," Mr. Jennings said. "We took the first plane out!"

Freddie ran to Jeff and hugged him. "Jeff! I knew you were innocent!"

Jeff smiled. "I never thought anyone would believe me! Those crooks had originally hired me to be a chauffeur. And I was broke enough to take any job I could find. At first, I had no idea that my driving job made me an accomplice to crime! I thought I was just working for some nice Americans who had moved to Nepal. By the time I found out they were crooks, they had already set me up so that I was the only one the police could identify. I tried to hide, but the thieves found me and threatened to kill me if I didn't drive the car."

"No charges were filed against Jeff," Mr. Manadhar said.

Jeff nodded. "Luckily, I overheard the thieves discussing a market in America for the statues. In fact, the man and woman had just returned from selling the statues there."

"And thanks to my son," Mr. Jennings said, "the police were able to locate the statues, which the American government will return."

Nan shuddered. "This must have been awful for you!"

"We knew there was a reason," Freddie said, "for the way your house looked! Broken dishes and all that mess!"

"How do you know what my house looked like?" Jeff asked.

"We went there looking for you," Flossie explained. "We tried to feed your kitty, but noticed she had already been fed."

"*He* had been fed," Jeff replied. "Poor kitty's been lonely while I've been out hiding. I've only had him a couple of weeks as it is. He was a little stray I took in."

"He'll be glad to have you home," Bert said.

Mr. Jennings looked his son in the eye. "Jeff, *we'd* be glad to have you come home— to your real home. Your mother and I, well, we've learned a valuable lesson. You're an adult now, and we promise to always treat you as the fine, mature man you are."

Mrs. Jennings wiped a tear from her eye. "Please, Jeff. We've missed you so!"

Jeff hugged them both. "I'd like nothing better. I've missed you just as much!"

"I'll miss you, Randy," Lakshmi said. "But if you go, can I have your cat?"

The Bobbsey family, the Manadhars, and Dorje and Rinpoche followed a servant through the elaborate marble palace. They gazed in awe at plush tapestries and statues. In the middle of a hall, a marble statue spouted water into a fountain.

After winding through several hallways, they were led into the throne room. They bowed and curtsied to the king and queen of Nepal. The queen was beautiful in a pink and gold silk sari, with brilliant jewels around her neck. The king was simply dressed in a Nepali hat, a navy-blue tunic, and white cotton pants.

"I want to personally thank you children," King Mahendra said, "for the excellent service you have rendered our country. Please approach the throne."

The children walked, one at a time, to the royal couple. Beautiful Queen Ratna hung gold medallions, engraved with pictures of the king and queen, around the neck of each child.

"Again, thank you," Queen Ratna said softly. "Stopping the thieves has meant a great deal to our people. You children are very good detectives! We won't forget any of you!"

"Yes," the king added, "thanks to you, the statues will soon be restored to their temples. All of Nepal is celebrating."

Queen Ratna turned to Mr. and Mrs. Bobbsey. "If you'd like to stay in Nepal longer, you'd be welcome as guests of the State."

"Thank you," said Mrs. Bobbsey, beaming with pride, "but we need to get home soon. Our plane leaves tonight, and the Jenningses are expecting to fly home with

us. But we're very grateful for the invitation."

Freddie had one question. "Mom and Dad," he said, "could you lend me money to buy film? The kids are all waiting for me at the temple."

Mr. Bobbsey laughed. "Son," he said, "if the king can give you a solid gold medal, the least I can do is treat you to the film!"